Disney's
The
PARENT
TRAP

A novel by Hallie Marshall
Based on the motion picture from Walt Disney Pictures
Screenplay by David Swift and Nancy Meyers
& Charles Shyer
Produced by Charles Shyer
Directed by Nancy Meyers

DISNEY
PRESS

New York

1986

It was a night of drifting clouds and a crescent moon, an elegant night on an elegant ship—the Queen Elizabeth 2. *In a carefully appointed dining room, it was a night for silk and candlelight, for white tablecloths and red wine, for fine crystal goblets and tuxedoed waiters, for gardenias and roses. And for one man and one woman, it was a night for love, for exchanging promises and wedding rings. It was a perfect night, but that was then. . . .*

Chapter 1
11 Years and 9 Months Later

A caravan of three buses threaded along a tree-lined road in Maine. Like stately clockwork, each turned up a narrow lane to pass through a wooden gate, freshly painted for the summer. This was the entrance to Camp Walden. Within was the green of the forest and the cool sparkle of a lake. A gathering of canoes waited patiently on the shore. And into this serene place drove the buses, honking, announcing their arrival. The first day of camp had begun.

From the buses poured girls, all sorts of girls, all shapes and sizes and styles of girls. There were lots and lots of girls, a noisy, messy confusion of girls. Teenage counselors were trying, without much luck, to control the pandemonium. As the bus drivers unloaded the cargo bays, tossing duffel bags and luggage into a disorganized pile, the general chaos mounted. It was time for the owner and director of the camp to take charge.

"Good afternoon, ladies, and welcome to Camp Walden," Marva Kulp, the senior Marva, yelled into a bullhorn. "I'm Marva Kulp, your camp director. Girls, let's find our duffels as quick as we can. We've got a big, big first day ahead of us."

The noise dimmed a decibel or so, and Marva nodded toward her daughter, a younger version of herself. "I'd like to turn the bullhorn over to my right-hand man, Marva Junior. Marva, bunk assignments, if you please."

Marva Junior took the bullhorn, pushed her glasses farther up on her nose, and began to bark out the assignments. "Okay, here we go. Listen up! Berg, Kate: Iroquois. Berg, Lily: Chickasaw. Burnham, Daisy: Kickapoo."

As the amplified voice of Marva Junior droned on, eleven-year-old Hallie Parker regarded the mountain of duffel bags. Somewhere within it was hers. Hallie wore plaid shorts, a green T-shirt, and a jean jacket. Her ears were pierced, she had shoulder length red hair, and she wore metallic blue polish on her fingernails.

Hallie had a habit of biting her nails, and also of talking to herself. She was talking to herself now. "Okay, found my duffel. But the question is—how do I get it out?" She took hold of the strap and said, "Okay, I can do it." She pulled. "Okay, no, I can't."

A skinny girl wearing glasses joined Hallie. "I'm Zoe," she said. "You must be new."

"How can you tell?" Hallie gave the strap another tug.

"You didn't know to grab your bag before the apes tossed it into the heap," Zoe told her. "I would say you need some serious help."

"Thanks," Hallie said. "It's the big yellow one."

Together, they struggled to free the bag. As the drivers tossed more duffels atop the pile, a girl wearing beads and a tie-dyed shirt lifted her bag from the center.

"Yo! Tie-dye girl!" Zoe shouted. The girl turned to face them.

"Could you give me a hand with my duffel?" Hallie called. "It's buried." The girl sauntered back and deliberately unloaded her duffel on Zoe's foot.

With one strong yank, the girl pulled Hallie's bag free.

"I'm Nicole," the girl informed her. "And you're welcome." She glanced down at the name tag on Hallie's duffel. "You're from California?"

"You are?" Zoe chimed in. "Do you live in Hollywood?"

"Do you, like, live next door to a movie star?" asked Nicole.

Hallie laughed. "What are you two—Lucy and Ethel? I've never even been to Hollywood. I live in Napa, in *northern* California, right next door to a vineyard."

"A what-yard?" Nicole asked.

"A vineyard," Hallie repeated. "It's where you make wine. That's what we do, me and my dad, we own a vineyard. What bunk are you guys in?"

In unison, the two girls answered, "Arapaho." They stared at each other, not exactly thrilled.

Then Hallie heard her name called over the bullhorn. "Parker, Hallie. . . . Parker, Hallie!"

"Right here!" Hallie put up her arm and waved.

"Arapaho," Marva Junior announced. "Bunk eleven."

Zoe offered her hand and Hallie slapped it. Then the three girls picked up their bags and headed toward the bunkhouse. On the way, Hallie had a question. "Either of you by any chance know how to play poker?"

When the others shook their heads, Hallie thought it

over. "No? Gee, what a shame. So, uh, tell me . . . how much cash did you guys bring with you this summer?"

Just then a long black limousine pulled through the gates and passed the girls. Hallie took one look at the limo and said, "Wow! Who's in there?"

Chapter 2

The driver of the limo hopped smartly out to open the rear door. A man in a proper suit stepped out. He spoke with a British accent, beautifully inflected. He was Martin, the butler.

The butler leaned in to take the hand of a well-dressed girl. Annie James, eleven years old, emerged from the limo. She had on an elegant powder-blue suit. A matching headband held back her long hair. She carried a vanity case, the smallest piece within a set of expensive luggage and a small navy purse.

As unlikely as it seemed, Annie James bore a remarkable resemblance to Hallie Parker.

"Well, here we are . . . Camp Walden for Girls." The butler looked about with disdain. "For this we traveled all the way from London?"

"It's rather picturesque, Martin. Don't you think?" Annie said with an English accent.

"I don't know if that's precisely the term I would use." Martin was still disapproving. "Let's review your mother's list. Shall we?" He flourished a typewritten sheet of paper. "Vitamins?"

"Check," Annie said.

"Minerals?"

"Check."

"List of daily fruits and vegetables?"

"Check, check," Annie responded. "Check fruits. Check vegetables. Go on."

"Herbal teas? Sun block? Lip balm? Insect repellent? Umbrella? Stationary? Stamps? Flashlight and batteries? Photos of your mother, your grandfather, and of course your trusty butler—me."

Annie smiled at him. "Got it all. I think."

Martin drew something from the pocket of his jacket. "Here's a little present from your grandfather, a spanking new deck of cards. Maybe you'll actually find someone on this continent who can whip your tush at poker."

"I doubt it." Annie grinned. "But thanks. And thanks for bringing me, Martin."

Martin looked away suddenly, blinking back his emotion. He grabbed Annie and hugged her tightly, then tried to regain his dignity. "Remember, if you change your mind and want me to collect you, I'm only a phone call away."

"I'll be fine," she assured him. "See you in eight weeks, Marty ol' pal."

"Missing you already," Martin told her, "queen of my heart."

Annie put out her hand and Martin shook it. They performed an extravagant secret handshake, complete with fancy claps and even a funny butt bump. When it was over, Martin resumed his place in the limousine and waved goodbye to Annie. As the vehicle pulled away, Annie waved back, excited to begin her first day at camp.

* * *

That night, every girl in the camp, each wearing a Camp Walden uniform, was gathered in the mess hall. Two lines of girls waited their turns at the buffet table. Hallie was in one line, and Annie was in the other. Annie grinned at her bunkmates and new friends, Jackie and Crosby, good eggs both. In the opposite line, Hallie was smiling at something Nicole had said to Zoe. They were all getting along just fine.

As Annie made it to the front of the line, she stood right next to Hallie for a split second. But Marva Senior stepped between them with a plate heaped high with food. "Excuse me, girls," she apologized. "I've just got to have a scoop of these gorgeous strawberries." She turned to Hallie. "Care for some?"

"Oh, no, thanks," Hallie said. "I'm allergic."

Marva Senior looked at Annie. "How 'bout you, dear? Strawberries?"

"Sorry." Annie shrugged. "I wish I could, but I'm allergic."

"Yes, yes, allergic. You just told me that." Confused, Marva Senior looked over to where Hallie had been, but she was gone. "How'd you get over there?" Marva asked Annie. "Oh, well, it's the first day of camp. You'll hafta forgive the ol' girl."

Marva was clearly confused. "At least I'm not putting salt in the sugar shakers yet. I mean, sugar in the salt . . ." Her voice trailed off as she realized that Annie, too, was gone. "Now where'd *she go*?"

Chapter 3

"*En garde!*" Two girls, each wearing a vest and a wire-mesh mask, were fencing. It was an uneven match. One of the duelers knocked the sword from the other's grasp, then knocked her on the grass. "*Touche!*" Marva Junior called out.

The girls took off their masks. It was Hallie who had won. Marva Junior took Hallie's arm and raised it in victory. "The winner and still undefeated champ . . . from Napa, California . . . Miss Hallie Parker!"

Hallie bowed and grinned proudly at Zoe and Nicole. And, at that moment, Annie and her friends arrived. "Do we have any challengers?" Marva Junior was asking. "C'mon, girls! Let's not be damsels in distress."

Annie spoke quietly. "I'll take a whack at it."

"Okay!" Marva Junior crowed. "We've got ourselves a challenger!"

Hallie slipped her mask back on and turned to confront her opponent. Annie, dressed now in vest and mask, flipped her sword skillfully into the air, caught it, and saluted. After a small hesitation, Hallie did the same.

"*En garde!*" Marva Junior blew her camp whistle. Hallie lunged. Annie parried, then attacked. Point for Annie.

Hallie came in low, executing a perfect offense. Point for Hallie. But with the next move, it was Annie who had the

advantage. She swept her sword full circle and brought the other girl close. They were mask to mask, then they broke apart.

The duel was growing heated. They were a perfect match. The other campers were cheering, going wild, as Annie forced Hallie back, back, back and into a water trough. Hallie landed, rear-end first, with a tremendous splash. The audience exploded with laughter.

Annie extended her hand to Hallie, intending to help her out. But Hallie yanked her into the trough. The girls sat in the water, soaked through, side by side.

"Looks like we got ourselves a new camp champ!" Marva Junior yelled. "From London, England . . . Miss Annie James! Okay, girls, shake hands."

The girls pulled off their masks and stood back to back.

"Cmon girls," Marva Jr. urged. "Shake hands." The girls reluctantly turned to face each other and froze. It was as if each was confronting a mirror. They frowned and crammed their hands into their pockets, at the exact same time. Their friends gathered around, looking from one to the other. No one knew what to say. "Why's everyone staring?" Hallie asked.

"Don't you see it?" Annie was incredulous. "The resemblance between us?"

"Resemblance? Between you and me?" Hallie examined her rival. "Well, your eyes are much closer together than mine. Your ears—well, you'll grow into them. Your teeth are a little crooked and that nose—well, those things can be fixed."

13

Zoe and Nicole laughed, and Jackie and Crosby got mad. "Want me to deck her for you?" Jackie asked Annie.

"Hold on," Hallie commanded. "I'm not quite finished. You want to know the real difference between us?"

Annie pretended unconcern. "Uh, let *me* see," she started in, "I know how to fence and you don't? Or I have class and you don't? Take your pick."

Marva Junior stepped between them. "Okay, time to break up this little love fest. Annie . . . Hallie . . . I mean Annie. . .Hallie?" The counselor had lost track of who was who. It was all too confusing. Besides, the lunch bell was ringing.

Jackie and Crosby linked arms with Annie, and Zoe and Nicole went with Hallie. "That girl," Hallie told them, "is a major loser."

"Yeah," Nicole agreed. "Too bad you couldn't look like somebody cooler."

Just then, Annie was asking her friends. "Do you think we look alike?"

"It's just a freak of nature." Crosby answered. "Please accept my condolences."

As they made their ways toward the dining hall, Annie looked at Hallie who was sneaking a look in her direction. Both girls looked away.

Annie spread her cards so the others could see them. "Sorry, ladies. Read 'em and weep." She swept the poker winnings into the pile in front of her. There were nickels and dimes, dollar bills, candy bars, hair clips. "So? No more takers?"

"You've already tooken everybody," one of the little kids said.

"Not quite everybody." The voice was Hallie's, and her eyes were confident.

Hallie shuffled and dealt, drew two, bluffed, and raked in the pot. Annie scooped the next. Back and forth, Annie won, then Hallie, and Hallie again, until Annie was down to her last dollar. "Three bucks," Hallie said. "I call."

Annie bit her lip. She was holding a good hand, but couldn't cover the bet. "Tell you what I'm gonna do," Hallie told her. "I'll make you a little deal. Loser jumps into the lake after the game."

Annie peeked at her cards. "Excellent," she replied.

Hallie had one more condition. "Butt-naked."

"Start unzipping, Parker," Annie said. "I have a straight—in diamonds."

Hallie smiled. "You're good, but not good enough. I have a royal flush."

Annie James had lost. Shivering, she removed her camp uniform and made her way to the dock. She took a breath, and dove bravely into the freezing water.

Annie had honored the bet. But when she swam to shore, her clothing was gone, and so were Hallie and her friends. "Fine!" Annie spoke with lips that were blue with cold. "If that's the way you want it . . . let the games begin."

Chapter 4

Hallie, Zoe, and Nicole were sweaty and worn out. The morning's hike had almost done them in, but their spirits were high. "I swear I heard your evil clone sneezing all the way across the mess hall," Zoe claimed.

Hallie sang, "That's the way, uh-huh, uh-huh, I like it!"

The other girls laughed, and Hallie stifled a yawn. "I'm tired," she announced. "I'm crawling back into bed and sleeping till lunch."

Nicole stopped short. "That does not seem like a possibility, babe."

Hallie and Zoe looked up. Every cot in bunk eleven was settled cozily on the roof. Hallie's mouth dropped open. "No way."

That night, three shadowy figures stole toward the Navajo bunkhouse. While Annie and her friends slept, the three intruders worked quickly. A jar of honey was poured into a pair of shoes. A can of shaving cream was squirted into a pillowcase. Twine wound crazily around the room. Cooking oil went on the floor. And a can of chocolate syrup was emptied into a bucket.

Reveille the next morning brought on a good show. As the Navajos awakened, they encountered the twine, the sticky honey, the oil. Dripping with shaving cream, Annie yelled, "That girl is without a doubt the lowest, most awful creature that ever walked the earth."

That girl was watching it all happen through the windows. "Thank you," Hallie acknowledged the compliment. "Thank you very much." She and Zoe and Nicole were pink from pent-up laughter. They slapped hands as the two Marvas approached, clipboards at the ready.

"Good morning, girls," Marva Senior greeted them.

"Morning, Marvas." The girls responded automatically. *"Marvas!?"*

Marva Senior climbed the steps to the bunkhouse. "Navajos!" she barked. "Surprise inspection! Ten-shun!" She reached for the handle to the screen door, but Hallie was blocking the way.

"No, Marva, don't go in there." Hallie thought fast. "One of the girls got sick and it's a big mess. Save yourself the aggravation. It's really disgusting."

Marva Senior blinked. "Well, if someone's sick, dear, then I must go in." She reached for the handle again, and Hallie tried to stop her. Above the doorway was perched the bucket with chocolate syrup. The Marvas were about to get it.

"No, really," Hallie begged, her eyes on the swaying bucket, "I can't let you go in. She's highly contagious."

"Actually," Annie's voice interrupted, "we're all quite fine in here. Unless Hallie Parker knows something we don't." Annie looked above the door and said, "Really, I insist, open the door and come see for yourself, ma'am."

17

Marva Senior swung the door open. Marva Junior was right behind her. A string attached to the door frame tipped the bucket of syrup over. Both Marvas were covered with chocolate. Screaming, they slipped on the oily floor, got tangled in the twine, and triggered another tilting bucket. One filled with feathers. The feathers floated down like a snowstorm and stuck to the honey and chocolate.

Hallie was aghast. "I told you it was a mess in there!"

Annie stood with her hands on her hips. "She should know. She did it!"

Marva Senior coughed up a few feathers and wiped the chocolate syrup from around her eyes. She focused on Annie and Hallie. "You and you. Pack your bags."

Annie and Hallie followed the Marvas up a steep hillside. Hallie balanced her yellow duffel on her shoulder, and Annie trudged along behind, her arms full of matched luggage. The entire camp marched behind them.

At the end of the path, Marva Senior blew her whistle and dismissed the other campers. "The rest of you go on back to your activities. You two—" She gestured toward a lonely cabin perched on top of the hill. "The isolation bunk."

The interior of the isolation bunk was as forlorn as the location. Sunlight illuminated the dust and the spider webs. "We've got six weeks left of camp," Marva Senior said. "And you two, who refuse to get along, are going to spend every glorious one of them together."

Marva Junior smirked. It was ghastly.

"You'll eat together," the senior Marva went on, "you'll bunk together and do all of your activities together. Either you'll find a way to get along or you'll punish yourselves far better than we ever could."

They exercised together, fenced and boxed together, read and played games together, shared meals—all without speaking. At bedtime, Hallie snuggled down with her stuffed animal, Cuppy, while Annie wrote letters. Hallie would reach up to switch off the lights, and Annie would snap them back on.

From the main lodge below, the Marvas could see the lights go off in the isolation bunk, then on, then off. On. Off. On. Off. On. The punishment was working.

Chapter 5

Thunder grumbled in the distance. It was pouring rain. Lightning flashed off the shabby walls of the isolation bunk. Hallie, in flannel pajamas and a sweatshirt, was pinning postcards and photos above her cot. Annie played solitaire. Now and then, they sneaked glances at each other.

A gust of sudden wind sent Hallie's photos flying. Together, the girls rushed to secure the windows. Then Annie bent to pick up Cuppy. "Anything ruined?" she asked.

Hallie held up a damaged photo. "Only the beautiful Leo DiCaprio."

"Who?"

"You've never heard of Leonardo DiCaprio?" Hallie couldn't believe it. "How far away is London, anyway?"

Annie calculated. "From here, three thousand miles. But sometimes, it seems farther. How far away is your home?"

"California's way at the other end of the country." Hallie held out another photograph. "Here's a picture of my house. We've got this incredible porch and—"

Annie wasn't paying attention. She was pointing to a man in the picture. His back was to the camera. "Who's that?"

"That's my dad. He's kinda like my best friend. We do everything together." Hallie looked over at Annie. "What's the matter?"

Annie rubbed at the goose bumps on her arms. "It's chilly in here, that's all."

Annie seemed a little spooked. It may have been the storm. Hallie went to her trunk to get some comfort food. She offered the bag to her bunkmate. "Oreos?"

"I love Oreos," Annie said. "At home I eat them with peanut butter."

"That's so weird," Hallie said. "So do I."

"You're kidding!" Annie laughed. "Most people find that disgusting."

"I know," Hallie agreed. "I don't get it." She rummaged around and found a jar of peanut butter. She passed it to Annie, and asked, "What's your dad like?"

"I don't have a father, actually." Annie took a bite of an Oreo and peanut butter. "I mean, I had one once, I suppose, but my parents divorced years ago."

Hallie shook her head. "It's scary the way nobody stays together anymore."

"Tell me about it," Annie said.

"How old are you?" Hallie asked.

"I'll be twelve on October eleventh."

Hallie choked on a mouthful of cookie. "So will I."

Annie was shocked. "Your birthday is October eleventh? How weird is that?"

"Extremely," said Hallie. "Hey, it stopped raining. Want to get a popsicle or something?"

The girls stepped out on the porch. Annie was studying Hallie—really looking her up and down as she toyed with her locket. Annie asked, "Hallie? What's your mother like?"

"I never met her," Hallie replied. "She and my dad split up when I was a baby. He doesn't talk about her, but I know she was beautiful. He had this old picture of her hidden in his sock drawer, and he gave it to me to keep. I'm really thirsty, are you sure you don't want to go to the mess hall and get a lemonade or something?"

"Will you stop thinking of your stomach at a time like this! Don't you realize what's happening?" Annie shook her head in disbelief. "Isn't it incredible that we look alike and have the same birthday? This is beyond coincidence! This is beyond imagination!"

Annie was talking a mile-a-minute, thinking aloud. "I only have a mother. You only have a father. You have one old picture of your mom. I have one old picture of my dad. But at least yours is probably a whole picture."

Hallie stood stock-still for a moment, then went over to her trunk. Annie explained, "The picture I have is pathetic. All crinkled and ripped right down the middle . . . " She paused to gaze at Hallie. "What are you looking for?"

"This," Hallie said. She held a photograph against her chest. "It's the picture of my mom. And it's ripped, too. Right down the middle."

Annie went to her dresser and took out a torn picture. "This is so freaky," she said. "On the count of three, we'll show them to each other. Okay?"

Hallie nodded. She counted along with Annie, "One . . . two . . . "

"Three!" The girls held their two pieces together and they made a whole photograph. A man and a woman were

22

sitting side by side. Behind them was a life preserver with the name of a ship written on it, the QE2.

"That's my dad," Hallie cried.

Annie added, "That's my mom."

They looked at the picture, then at each other. When the lunch bell rang, neither moved. "I'm not so hungry any more." Hallie swallowed hard. "So, if your mom is my mom and my dad is your dad . . . then we're . . . like . . . sisters."

"Sisters?" Annie was in shock. "We're like . . . twins!" Tears came to her eyes. She reached out to hug Hallie. Hallie was crying, too.

After a while, they drew apart. They both smiled and began to laugh. Hallie's hand went to something around her neck. "What's that?" Annie asked.

"My locket," Hallie said. "I got it when I was born. It has an 'H' on it."

"I got mine when I was born, too." Annie showed her own locket to Hallie. "Only mine has an 'A' on it."

"Now *I've* got goose bumps," Hallie exclaimed. "Ohmygod! I'm not an only child! I'm a twin! There's two of me . . . two of us . . . this is like . . . "

"Mind-boggling," Annie finished.

"Totally," Hallie said. "Ohmygod."

"Ohmygod," Annie echoed.

Chapter 6

A crescent moon was cradled in a starry sky. The girls had taped their parents photos together and pushed their cots side-by-side in the isolation bunk. They were talking quietly. in the dark. Hallie asked, "Tell me, what's Mom like?"

"She designs wedding gowns," Annie told her. "She's becoming quite famous, actually. A princess in Greece just bought one of her gowns."

Hallie was impressed. "Wow."

Annie asked, "Has Dad ever been close to getting re-married?"

"No." Hallie shook her head. "He always says I'm the only girl in his life."

"Mom's never come close either. Do you think, secretly, in their innermost hearts, they're still in love with each other?"

Hallie sighed. "If they're still in love, why haven't they seen each other?"

"That's the way true love works." Annie propped herself up on an elbow. "History is filled with stories of lovers parted by some silly misunderstanding."

Then Hallie sat bolt upright. "I have a brilliant beyond brilliant idea. I'm a total genius. You want to know what Dad is like, right?"

"Right." Annie was staring at her.

"Okay. And I'm dying to know Mom. I'm thinking we

should switch places. When camp's over I go to London as you, and you go to California as me. Annie, we can pull it off," Hallie insisted. "We're twins, aren't we?"

"Twins from different countries, with different accents, different hairstyles, different vocabularies . . . different everything," Annie pointed out.

"I'll teach you to be me, and you teach me to be you." Hallie pursed her lips and imitated Annie perfectly, "*You* want to know the difference between us? I have *class* and you don't."

Annie winced. Hallie sounded just like her. But Annie was coming around, and she was thinking ahead. "The truth is, you know, that if we switch . . . sooner or later, they'll have to unswitch us."

Hallie grinned. "And when they do, they'll have to meet again. Face to face."

"After all these years," Annie added.

"Thank you," Hallie said. "I told you I'm brilliant."

"Okay. This is Grandfather." Annie passed a photograph to Hallie.

"He's so cute," Hallie said. "What do we call him?"

"Grandfather," Annie answered simply. She handed over another photo. "This is Martin. He's our butler."

"We have a butler?" Hallie crowed. "How cool!"

The walls of the isolation bunk were covered with charts and diagrams of Annie's home in London and Hallie's place in Napa. Each had been carefully memorized, and the girls no longer needed them. "Okay. I'm ready." Annie shut her eyes.

25

Hallie hesitated, comb in hand, scissors at the ready. She grabbed a clump of Annie's hair and closed her eyes, as well.

Annie peeked. "Don't shut *your* eyes!"

"Oh, right. Sorry," Hallie apologized. "I'm a little nervous."

"*You're* nervous!" Annie snorted. "Go ahead, just do it!"

Hallie raised the scissors and sliced away until there was a ring of hair laying on the floor. When Annie confronted her "new" style in the mirror, she saw a reflection of Hallie. The girls were now identical in every way. "This is scary," Annie said.

"Honey, you never looked better." Then Hallie exclaimed, "Ohmygod!"

Annie glanced in the mirror again. "What?"

"I have pierced ears," Hallie told her.

Annie panicked. "Oh, no. Forget it. Not happening. I won't. I refuse."

There was the scratch and flare of a match. Hallie held a needle into the flame. Calmly, she reported, "Needle sterilized."

Annie held an ice cube against her ear. "You know what you're doing?"

"Relax," Hallie said. "I've gone with all my friends to have their ears pierced. Just close your eyes, and it'll all be over before you know it. Earring ready?"

In reply, Annie held up one of Hallie's earrings. "On the count of three," Hallie instructed, "remove the ice. One . . . two . . . three!"

Annie squeezed her eyes tightly shut as Hallie stuck the needle through her earlobe. Both girls screamed.

Chapter 7

The buses were lined up and waiting. Crosby, Jackie, Zoe, and Nicole hugged the twins good-bye, exchanged addresses, promised to write. Hallie was dressed in Annie's suit, and Annie was wearing Hallie's shorts and jean jacket. No one could tell them apart.

"Okay, so you're going to find out how Mom and Dad met . . . " Annie started.

". . . And you're gonna find out why they broke up," Hallie finished for her.

"Annie James! Annie James!" Marva Junior was shouting into her bullhorn. "Annie James! Your car is here!"

Annie looked at Hallie. "That's you. Here's your ticket and your passport. Martin will pick you up at the airport tomorrow morning."

"Annie James!" Marva yelled. "Last call for Annie James!"

"Give Mom a kiss for me," Annie said.

"And give Dad one from me," said Hallie.

"Okay, this is it," Hallie was talking to herself as the plane approached the runway. She was about to land in London. "Oh, God, I hope she likes me. Please like me."

A stream of passengers swept through the terminal. Hallie was frightened but excited, too, and definitely feeling

27

lost, when she heard a name being called. "Annie! Annie!"
It was Martin.

"Maaw-tin!" Hallie responded with her best British accent.
She ran to hug him, grateful the butler had found her.

"What did you do to your hair?" Martin asked.

"Cut it. Do you like it?"

"Love it!" he said. "It's the new you! And you've had your
ears pierced. Give me five, girlfriend!"

Martin put out his hand to start the secret handshake.
Hallie drew a blank for a moment, then remembered the
moves Annie had taught her. She executed them to perfection.

"This is so amazing. What a city!" The sights and sounds of
London were fascinating. From the backseat of the Bentley,
Hallie was having a hard time keeping her comments to herself.

Martin shook his head. "Eight weeks at camp and suddenly you're acting like an American tourist."

"That's what camp's for, silly." Hallie was fast thinking of
an excuse. "Makes you appreciate home."

Chapter 8

The diagrams Annie had drawn hadn't done justice to the eighteenth-century town home, the shade and light, the elegance, the lovely street. "This is it," Hallie said to herself. "Seven Pembroke Lane."

She stood in the foyer and gathered her courage. "Hello!" she called. "Hello?" She peeked into the drawing room, then into the library. Someone was there, hidden behind the *Financial Times*. "Grandfather! I'm home,"

Charles James put down his paper with a smile. "Is that my little girl?" Hallie swallowed hard. "Yes, it's me."

Her grandfather hugged her tight. "Did you have a good time?" he asked. "What are you doing?"

"Smelling," Hallie told him. "Years from now, when I'm all grown-up, I'll remember my grandfather, and how he smelled of peppermint and pipe tobacco."

He tightened his hold and Hallie rested her head on his chest. Then she heard someone calling. "Annie! Annie!"

It was her mother. Hallie stood as if in a trance, taking in her beauty, her grace, her mother. At last she said, "I can't believe it's you."

"And I can't believe it's you," Elizabeth said. She took Hallie into her arms. "And with short hair! Who cut it for you?"

"A girl I met at camp," Hallie told her. "Do you hate it?"

"I love it." said her mother, "And you got your ears pierced!"

Elizabeth held Hallie at arm's length. "Any other surprises? A belly-button ring? A tattoo?" Hallie was crying. "Darling?" her mother said. "What is it?"

"I'm sorry," Hallie sobbed. "It's just . . . that . . . I've missed you so much."

Her mother brushed back a lock of Hallie's hair. "I know. It seems like it's been forever."

"You have no idea," Hallie said.

Hallie took in everything. The portraits that lined the hallway, her mother's sitting room. An afternoon tea had been set on a table in the corner. "Ohmygod," Hallie exclaimed. "I love this room. It's so totally mom-like."

Elizabeth looked around. "Nothing's new. It's as mom-like as it's always been. So, come on, tell me about camp. Did you like everyone? Was it fun?"

"It was great. I liked this one girl a real lot—I mean, in particular. She's from California." Hallie paused to let that sink in. "Have you ever been to California?"

"Yes. Once," her mother answered. "But that was a long time ago. Before you were born."

Martin came in, holding Cuppy by one ear. "I found a stowaway in your suitcase," he informed Hallie.

"Ohmygod, Cuppy!"

"Cuppy?" Elizabeth questioned.

Hallie turned to her mother quickly. "He belongs to my

friend. The one I was telling you about. I can't imagine how he got in my suitcase."

"Well, since he's not *our* Cuppy, shall we dispose of the little creature?" Martin's tone held disgust.

"No!" Hallie cried. "I'll mail, I mean post, I'll send him to her. She loves this thing a lot. A lot. She could never be in . . . like . . . in a foreign country without him."

Martin gave her a puzzled glance, but Hallie was saved by the bell. The telephone rang, and Elizabeth went to answer it. "Hello? Oh. How's the photo shoot going? Oh. Can't you manage? Annie just got home from camp. Oh."

While Elizabeth was talking, Hallie examined the things on the dresser, her mother's brush, her pearls, her perfume. And when her mother hung up the phone, she asked if Annie wanted to go to the studio with her.

Hallie did, of course. She walked down the street with her mother, feeling supremely happy. She looked into windows of shops as they passed, until they came to one with a mannequin wearing an exquisite wedding gown. Above the window was a sign: ELIZABETH JAMES DESIGNS.

"Wow," Hallie said. "That's incredible. You designed that?"

"I had to do something while you were at camp." Her mother smiled. "You don't think it's too—?"

"It's gorgeous." Hallie was in awe. "I love it. You know who would look really beautiful in that gown? I mean, like, *really* beautiful? You."

"Me?" Elizabeth tapped her daughter on the forehead. "You know what? I think the time change has made you a little loopy. Come on. Let's see what the fuss is all about."

Chapter 9

"You mean you never think about getting married again?" Hallie had been at first distracted by the sights of the Bridal Boutique—the beautiful gowns, the vase of white orchids— but she wasn't giving up on her train of thought.

"No," Elizabeth's answer was clipped. "I like things exactly the way they are, thank you."

A woman hurried toward them with a veil. "Hi, Elizabeth. Hey, Annie! Welcome home. Great haircut."

"Thanks—" Hallie searched her memory, trying to remember the assistant's name. It came to her: "Fiona! Yeah, I'm back. But, Mom, seriously . . . "

"Seriously," her mother warned, "we have to get upstairs."

"Doesn't designing these gowns ever make you think about getting married again?" Hallie continued doggedly. "Or at least make you think about the 'F' word?"

Everyone in the room stopped what they were doing and looked up. "The 'F' word?" Elizabeth inquired cautiously.

"My *father*!"

"Oh. That 'F' word." Hallie's mother was relieved. "Well, no, it doesn't," and she lowered her voice. "I didn't even wear a wedding gown when I married the 'F' word. And how did we get into this discussion, anyway?"

Annie and Martin, the butler, say good-bye with their secret hand-shake.

Hallie and her partners in crime turn Annie's cabin into an obstacle course!

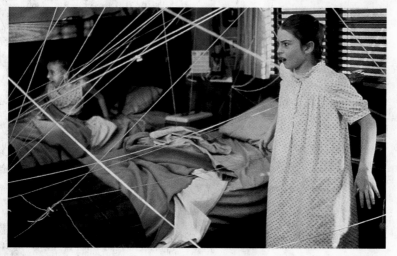

Uh, oh! The two Marvas step right into Hallie's chocolate syrup and feather trap.

"One . . . two . . . three . . ."—and the pictures complete the puzzle.

Hallie and Annie finalize their plot to switch places on their parents.

"Just do it," Annie orders as Hallie cuts off her long hair.

"I can't believe it's you," Hallie says as she sees her mother for the first time.

Far from London, Annie runs to hug the father she has never met.

Annie dives right into ranch life.

Hallie poses with one of her mom's wedding creations—and model Vendela!

"You listen good—I'm marrying your father in two weeks whether you like it or not," Meredith warns Annie.

The girls put their matchmaking plan into motion with their unsuspecting parents.

"When the camping trip is over, we'll tell you who's Hallie and who's Annie," the girls inform Nick and Elizabeth.

"It's *only* a lizard," Annie tells a horrified Meredith.

As soon as Nick turns his back, the girls prepare their plan to do away with Meredith.

"We finally did it!"

Elizabeth opened a set of double doors. A photo shoot was in progress. The photographer glanced up with relief. "Okay, she's here. We're saved."

"Sorry," the model apologized. "We don't know what to do with the veil."

"If she wears it, it covers the back of the dress," the photographer explained. "And if she doesn't wear it, the dress looks—"

"Incomplete," Elizabeth said. "You're right. Okay. I see the problem. Annie, darling, fetch me one of those top hats in the window."

After a slight hesitation, Hallie picked out a white hat and a black one from the display. "Which do you like?" her mother asked.

"The white one," Hallie answered.

"Me, too." Elizabeth smiled at Hallie and handed the white top hat to the model.

The model twirled around. "I love this," she said.

"Now, throw the veil straight back," Elizabeth advised. "Someone turn on the fan. Now, hold onto your hat. Don't worry about the bouquet and don't forget to look happy. It's your wedding day."

Hallie sighed with admiration and a smile spread across her face. "My mom is too cool."

"So what *did* you wear to marry my dad?" Though it was late afternoon, Hallie hadn't forgotten her mission. She and her mother were walking through a beautiful shopping arcade, but Hallie was too wound up to notice the surroundings.

33

"Why the sudden curiosity?" her mother asked.

"Well, maybe because you never mention him, and you can't blame a kid for wondering," Hallie said. "Mother, you can't avoid the subject forever. At least tell me what he was like."

Elizabeth gave in. "Okay. He was quite lovely, to tell you the truth. When we met, he was entirely lovely. All right?"

"All right." Hallie was pleased. "So did you meet him here in London?"

"We met on the QE2. It's an ocean liner that sails from London to New York." Elizabeth's voice went soft with memory. "We met our first night aboard. We were next to each other at dinner. He's an American, you know."

"No kidding?" Hallie prompted.

"We hit it off immediately." They emerged from the arcade and it was raining. Elizabeth snapped open her umbrella and held it over herself and Hallie.

"So was it love at first sight?"

Her mother looked down at her. "I knew you were going to ask me all these questions one day." She raised her arm and hailed a taxicab. It splashed to a stop and they got into the backseat together.

Hallie snuggled close, but she kept up the questions. "So did you see each other every single night?"

Elizabeth examined her daughter closely. "This part of your personality reminds me of your father. You'd think he brought you up instead of me."

Hallie felt a flash of worry, but then her mother answered, "Yes, we saw each other every night, every

34

morning, and every hour in between. One night, he popped the question. Right there in the middle of the Atlantic."

"That is so cool."

"Since a ship's captain can do all kinds of things, like even marry people—"

"Ohmygod," Hallie interrupted. "You mean you got married on the QE2? That is beyond cool! But what happened? You didn't love each other when you weren't in the middle of the Atlantic?"

"I don't know, honey. These things are complicated. I'm very English and your father is very American. I tried living in California and he tried living in London, but—" Elizabeth's voice faltered.

"But it just didn't work out."

"I'm afraid it didn't." Her mother kissed the top of her head. "Except for having you."

Hallie shut her eyes and felt the comfort of her mother's arms. "Dear old Dad," she whispered, "I wonder what he's doing at this very moment."

Chapter 10

Nick Parker was looking entirely lovely, indeed. He stood tall within the crowd at the Napa Airport, his eyes eager. "Welcome home, kiddo!"

Annie almost dropped Hallie's duffel bag. "Oh, gosh. It's him." She broke into a wild, wide smile and rushed toward him. "Dad!"

"Get into these arms, you little punk!" Her dad scooped her up.

Annie buried her face against his shoulder. "Dad . . . finally."

"I hope you had a lousy time at camp," he said, "because you're never going back. I missed you too much." He drew back and looked her over. "What happened to you, Hal? Something's changed. Did you get taller?"

Annie didn't answer. He put her down and they walked arm in arm out of the airport. She tested out leaning her head against him. "So what's up, Dad? How's Chessy and everybody?"

"Great. Everybody's great. They can't wait to see you. Eight weeks really is too long, Hal. So much has been happening around here."

"A lot has happened to me, too," Annie ventured. "I feel like a new woman."

Nick laughed. But as Annie kept peeking at him, he got self-conscious. "What's the matter? Did I cut myself shaving?"

"No, it's just that seeing you for the first time, the first time in a long time, I mean—" Annie giggled. "You look taller to me, too."

"C'mon, squirt. Let's go home." He held open the door to his truck. "By the way, thanks for all those newsy letters." Her father's eyes were bright beneath the shadowed brim of a cowboy hat. "I'm really glad I bought you that stationary."

Annie gazed out at the California countryside, at the clear skies and ordered vineyards. "We meant to write, Dad, but we just got so busy."

"We?"

"Oh. Me and my friend. I met this girl at camp and we got really close," Annie said. "Practically like sisters. She was a lovely girl."

"Lovely?" Nick repeated. "You seem to have gotten very proper all of a sudden." He took her hand and squeezed it. "Still biting those nails, I see."

"Dad!" she squealed. "You noticed!"

"Whaddya mean, noticed? You've been biting them since you could chew."

"But I've decided to stop, Dad. It's a horrid habit, really it is, Dad."

He sped up to pass a battered truck. "A 'lovely girl'? 'Horrid habit'? Did I send you to summer camp or finishing school? And why do you keep saying 'Dad' at the end of every sentence?"

"I'm sorry, I didn't realize I was doing it, Dad." Annie caught herself that time and laughed. "Do you want to know why I keep saying 'Dad'?"

"Because you missed your old man?"

"Exactly!" Annie said. "In my *whole* life—I mean, in the last eight weeks, I was never able to say the word 'Dad.' Never. If you ask me, a dad is an irreplaceable person in a girl's life. Just imagine a life without a father."

Annie was getting carried away, but she couldn't stop. "Never buying a Father's Day card, never getting your father a birthday present, never sitting on his lap, never being able to say 'Hi, Dad,' or 'What's up, Dad,' or 'Bye, Dad,' or 'Catch you later, Dad.' I mean, never—"

"Let me see if I get this," he interrupted finally. "You missed being able to call me *Dad*."

She smiled at him, warm and honest. "Yeah. I really have, Dad."

The house was a sprawling place with an inviting porch and a gravel driveway that crunched beneath the wheels. A big golden mutt, Sammy, barked from an upstairs window. And there was Chessy, running out the front door. Annie felt as if she'd known her forever.

"Hello, gorgeous!" Chessy's embrace lifted Annie off her feet. "You grew, you look fabulous, we missed you, but don't let your old man talk you out of going to camp next year. You need adventure. I made cornbread and chili. Why are you so quiet? What's wrong?"

Annie told the truth. "I'm just so happy to be home."

Nick shouldered the duffel bag and sniffed the air. "Did I hear chili?"

"It's on the stove." Chessy gave Annie a long look. "You've changed, Hal. I can't put my finger on it, but something has definitely changed."

"Really?" Annie asked in her best American accent. "It's just the same old me." To escape Chessy's scrutiny, Annie turned to the dog. "Hi, Sammy!"

It was a mistake. Sammy's tail went down. He backed off, growling suspiciously. "I probably smell like camp," Annie said. "That's all." She ran up the porch steps and disappeared inside.

Chessy stayed for a moment with Sammy. "What's with you, goofball?" she asked the dog. "It's like you didn't even recognize her."

Chapter 11

The interior of the house was lived in and loved, with high ceilings and windows that displayed the vineyard beyond. Annie wanted to stop and stare, but Chessy was right behind her. "Whaddya want to do first, kiddo? Unpack or eat? Or eat, then unpack? Or eat, while we unpack?"

"You mean I can eat in my room?"

Chessy looked at her as if she was nuts. "Yes, I would say that's a possibility."

To demonstrate, Annie's father came in, eating from a big bowl. "Hal? When you're done, come out to the pool. There's someone I want you to meet."

"Okay, Dad." Annie's smile faded as she saw who her father meant, a leggy woman with a big hat who joined Nick on the porch. She hadn't been in any of Hallie's pictures. "So, who's the blonde?" she asked Chessy.

Chessy busied herself with Hallie's duffel. "It's none of my business how your father makes a fool out of himself. He's a big boy; he can do what he wants."

"Okay, but who is she?" Annie tried to sound as flippant as Hallie.

"Her name is Meredith Blake. Your father hired her to do some publicity. but if you ask me, she's done a better job of selling herself than the grapes."

Annie felt a rise of fear. "What do you mean?"

"I kept wondering what a hot young thing like her sees in a guy who walks around with his shirttail hanging out and his cereal bowl full of chili." Chessy had a hard time meeting her eyes. "Then I realized there's a million reasons why that girl's giggling . . . and they're all sitting in the Napa Valley Community Bank."

Annie picked up a camera from the dresser. It had a zoom lens. She focused on Meredith who was giggling in the garden with *her* dad. "You mean, you don't think she really likes him."

"What do I know?" Chessy shrugged. "But this one could give Sharon Stone femme fatale lessons. She's got your father eating out of the palm of her hand. They ride together. They swim together. They're out to dinner every night."

Chessy began to sort through Hallie's clothes. "Plus, she treats me like 'the help.' Which has truly endeared her to me But you go meet her and see for yourself. Don't let me influence you."

Annie changed into a bathing suit and a faded Parker Vineyards T-shirt she found in Hallie's bureau and went out to the pool. "There's my girl!" her father said. "Hal, honey, this is Meredith Blake."

"Hi!" Meredith was wearing a wide-brimmed black hat. "Wow. I can't believe I'm finally meeting the famous Hallie. I've looked forward to this all summer."

"Really?" Annie's response was guarded. "Well, here I am."

"Nicky! She's adorable!" Meredith gushed. "The way

41

your father talked about you, I expected to meet a little girl. But you're so grown-up—"

"I'll be twelve soon," Annie said. "How old are you?"

Meredith was a little thrown, but she answered. "Twenty-six."

"Only fifteen years older than me. How old are you again, Dad?"

"Oh, suddenly she's interested in math." Nick smiled apologetically at Meredith. "I'm gonna get some more chili . . . and a bottle of champagne to celebrate."

Annie's eyes narrowed with suspicion. "What are we celebrating?"

Meredith jumped in right away. "Your homecoming. Of course."

As Nick headed back to the house, he and Meredith exchanged a warm glance that was not lost on Annie. She dangled her feet in the water and thought hard.

Meredith put on some lip gloss and flipped open her cellular phone. "Hello . . . Reverend Mosby . . . Of course I understand it's for a local charity . . . sounds very worthwhile . . . but unfortunately, Mr. Parker will be out of the country during that time."

Meredith mouthed some more excuses and snapped the phone shut. "My dad's going out of the country?" Annie asked her. "When?"

"Oh. I just had to tell a little white lie to get him out of something." Meredith changed the subject. "I've never heard a man talk about his daughter the way Nicky talks about you. You two are obviously incredibly close."

"We're closer than close. We're all each other has . . . "
Annie bunched herself up and cannonballed into the pool.
She splashed water all over Meredith. "Sorry. Did I get you
wet, Mer?"

"Just a little, Hal." Meredith patted her sleek face dry
with a towel. "Hey, guess what? Your daddy took me riding
the other day and he let me ride your horse."

"That's okay. Sprout's used to strange women," Annie
said. "Not that you're strange. Actually, compared to the
others, you seem relatively normal."

Meredith was curious. "What others?"

Annie shook her head sadly. "I guess I'd want to know if
I was number twenty-eight—I mean, twenty-nine—in a
man's life. But I couldn't count until I was about four. God
knows how many there were before then."

Meredith bought it. "I'm number twenty-nine?"

"It's always the same routine," Annie lied. "Horseback
riding through the vineyards, romantic dinners with his
special reserve–label wine . . . "

Meredith was nodding. Annie went on, "It's none of my
business if a man his age wants to make a fool out of himself. Maybe you're the real thing, Mer."

When Nick reappeared with a bottle of champagne in
his hand, Meredith smiled at him with an effort. "Here we
go," he said. "A bottle of my special reserve label. Did you
girls find something to talk about while I was gone?"

Annie winked at Meredith and dove smoothly beneath
the water. "Does that mean yes?" Nick asked.

"It sure does," Meredith said.

Chapter 12

The phone was ringing and Grandfather walked past it, absorbed in his morning paper. "Somebody grab that, please?" Elizabeth ordered from the top of the stairs. Martin rolled his eyes and rebalanced the tray of coffee he was carrying. He picked up the phone. "James residence. *Annie*? Is that you?" He did a double take when Hallie came in. "A Mildred Plotka for you, Annie. Sounds like your twin."

Hallie raised her eyebrows. "My twin? Very funny. Hello? Mildred!"

It was midnight in California. Annie was locked inside the bathroom. She spoke with her own accent. "Hey! How's it going over there?"

Hallie's accent was a duplicate of Annie's. "Everything's lovely here. We're expecting rain. Mildred, can you hold on for a moment?" Hallie ducked inside the hall closet. "Okay," she said. "Now I can talk."

She settled more comfortably among the jackets and coats and talked as herself. "Ohmygod, Mom's incredible! I cannot believe I've lived my entire life without knowing her. She's beautiful and fun and smart and—"

Annie whistled into the phone. "Hallie, stop! We've got a major problem. You're going to have to bring Mother out here immediately."

"Immediately? Are you nuts?" Hallie asked. "I've had one day with her. I'm just getting to know her. I can't. I won't."

"But this is an emergency!" Annie insisted. "Dad's in love."

Hallie laughed. "Get out of here! Dad doesn't fall in love. Not seriously."

"He's serious about this one. Always holding her hand, kissing her neck . . . "

"He is?" Hallie's heart sank. "You'll have to sabotage her. Do whatever you have to."

"I'm trying!" Annie was nearly yelling. "But I'm at a disadvantage—I only met the man twelve hours ago. You've got to get back here to help me."

"Annie, I can't. I want more time with Mom." Hallie found a candy wrapper in a coat pocket and crinkled it, making a sound like static. "Annie! Are you still there? I can barely hear you. Operator! Operator! Think I lost you, Ann."

The connection went dead and Annie glared at the receiver. "Thanks for your help, Hal."

Hallie emerged from the closet on her hands and knees. Her mother, grandfather, and Martin were all staring at her. "It's a camp tradition . . . talk from inside a closet . . . it's stupid . . . I know." She untangled the cord and replaced the phone. "Breakfast, anyone?"

Chessy put a full plate in front of Annie. "Here we go. Eggs, bacon, toast, and a stack of humongous chocolate-chip pancakes. Your dad wants you to go over to his office as soon as you're done eating."

"He does?" Annie shoved some toast in her mouth. "I'm done." She scooted her chair back and got up to go. Sammy growled at her. "That dog has gotten so weird," Annie said. "Bye, Chessy. Thanks again. Breakfast was great."

Chessy contemplated the mostly untouched food. She watched as Annie pulled on the screen door. "Push, Hal," Chessy instructed quietly. She followed the girl with troubled eyes as Annie ran from the house.

When Annie found her father, he put his arm around her. Together, they ambled through the room in which barrels of wine were stored. "Hal, I'm glad you're here. There's something really important I want to talk to you about."

"That's funny," Annie said. "Because there's something really important I want to talk to you about."

"Okay." He took a breath. "I want to talk to you about Meredith."

"And I want to talk to you about my mother," Annie put in quickly. Nick was surprised. "What about your mother?"

"Dad, I'm almost twelve. A girl needs more in life than half of a crumpled old photograph. Dad, face it . . . I need a mother."

It backfired. Nick just nodded. "You know what? You're right. Which brings me to—" They turned a corner and came face to face with her. "Meredith!"

Trotting at Meredith's heels was a man. "Hi, Hal," she said. "This is my assistant, Richard. Hallie is Nick's daughter, the one I've been telling you about."

"Oh, hello," he intoned in a stuffy accent. "How are you, luv?"

"Don't tell me you're British?" Annie's tone echoed his. "How lovely."

Nick's mouth dropped. "How'd you do that?" he asked Annie.

Richard complimented her. "You do an absolutely marvelous accent."

"Yours isn't so bad either, old chap," said Annie.

Behind him, Meredith nudged Nick and whispered, "Did you tell her?"

"Later," he said. He turned down Meredith's invitation to have lunch on the terrace, saying, "I promised Hal we'd hang out together this afternoon."

"No problem, " Meredith trilled. "I'm working on a new label design, Nicky. You're gonna love it. It features Y-O-U." She spelled the word and blew a kiss. "Bye, Hals!"

Under her breath, Meredith told her assistant, "First change I make in that household is to send that little brat off to boarding school in Timbuktu."

"Oooooooo!" Richard shivered. "Ice woman!"

"And proud of it," she said.

Chapter 13

Nick slowed his horse to a walk and leaned back in the saddle. "So, Hal, are you excited about our camping trip?"

"What camping trip?" Unlike Sammy, Sprout had been happy to see her.

"Our *camping* trip," he repeated. "The one we take every summer before you go back to school."

"Oh, *that* one." Annie wished Hallie had told her about it. "I can't wait."

He switched subjects abruptly. "What do you think of Meredith?"

"Well, she's cute," Annie said. "She has nice hair, good teeth, and can spell the word Y-O-U. Honestly, Dad, why do you want my opinion anyway?"

"Because—" His voice cracked. "Because, believe it or not, honey . . . because . . . "

Whatever it was, Annie knew it was something she didn't want to hear. She dug her heels into Sprout's flanks and the horse took off. "Race you back to the house, Dad!"

"Hallie!" He shouted after her. "I'm trying to tell you something!"

* * *

When she reached the house, Annie ran up the steps and threw open the screen door. "I can't handle this alone," she said out loud. "I just can't. I'm only one kid."

Chessy appeared from behind a chair. "You got something to share with the class, Hal?"

Annie jumped. "Oh, Chessy!" she exclaimed. "You gave me a fright!"

"You sure there's nothing you want to talk to me about?" Chessy's eyes were steady. "Like why Sammy never comes near you anymore, or why your appetite's changed, or why you're suddenly using expressions like "you gave me a fright'?"

"Chessy, I changed a lot over the summer," Annie said nervously. "That's all."

"If I didn't know better, I'd say it's almost as if you were—" Chessy pushed off the thought. "Oh, never mind. It's impossible."

Annie swallowed hard. "Almost as if I were *who*?"

"Nobody," Chessy snapped. "Forget I even mentioned it."

But Annie kept after it. "Almost as if I were . . . Annie?"

Chessy was stunned. "You know about Annie?"

"I *am* Annie," she said in a matter-of-fact-way. There it was, out in the open.

Suddenly, Nick burst in. "Why'd you take off like that? I told you I wanted to talk to you." He noticed Chessy was staring. "Chessy? Why are you looking at her like that?"

"Like what?" Chessy blurted out. "I'm looking at her just like I've looked at her for eleven years. Since the day she came home from the hospital, six pounds, eleven ounces, twenty-one inches long. . . . "

Chessy was crying, actually sobbing. "She's so beautiful and so big."

She hugged Annie and unsteadily left the room,

muttering about fixing a special feast in the kitchen. Nick watched in amazement. "Why's everybody acting so nutty around here? Hal, we gotta talk."

"Okay," Annie said. "Shoot."

"I want to know what you think about making Meredith part of the family."

"It's an awesome idea," Annie replied. "I've always wanted a big sister."

Nick choked. "Honey, I'm afraid you're kind of missing the point."

She grinned at him. "You're going to adopt Meredith. That is so sweet, Dad."

"I'm not going to *adopt* her, I'm going to *marry* her," he said.

"Marry her! That's insane! How can you marry a woman young enough to be my big sister?" Annie ranted and raved and slipped in a few bad words in French.

"Calm down!" Nick said, and then it hit him. "Now you speak French?"

"I learned it at camp," she lied once more. "Let's discuss this rationally."

"In English, if you don't mind," he insisted. "What has gotten into you?"

"Nothing. It's just—it's nothing. Dad, you can't get married!" she wailed. "It'll totally ruin completely everything!"

Annie stormed out, narrowly missing Chessy in the hallway. "Don't look at me," Chessy warned Nick. "I don't know a thing." She slammed the kitchen door.

There was the honk of a horn outside. It was Meredith announcing her arrival, rap music blasting from her car radio. "She thought I was going to *adopt* her?" Even Nick was talking to himself.

"Hi, doll!" Meredith swept onto the patio and sat down on Nick's lap. She ran her fingers through his hair. "You look stressed, baby. How about a martini?"

He sighed. "How about a double?"

Meredith opened her purse and brought out a Tiffany box. Inside was a silver bell. She rang it. "Don't you just love it? It's just what we need. It's such a big house!"

Chessy made an appearance, none too excited. "You rang?"

"Two martinis, please," Meredith ordered. "Make Mr. Parker's a double."

Chessy stood in place until Nick pressed his fingers to his temples. "Please, Chessy," he begged. "I'm getting a migraine."

Holding her shirttails out as if they formed a skirt, Chessy curtsied and left. Meredith said, "I don't know if a uniform will make her look better or worse."

It wasn't anywhere Nick wanted to go. "I told Hallie," he said at last. "She went ballistic. Started yelling in French, which I didn't even know she spoke. I just don't get her lately."

"Nick, this reaction is totally classic." Meredith massaged Nick's neck. "Look, why don't I talk with her . . . woman to woman."

Nick wasn't sure. "She's a little sensitive about you right now."

"That's why I need to do it. We've got to break the ice sometime."

Chapter 14

"Knock-knock! Can I join you?" Meredith plopped down across from Annie on her swing. "Guess the news of the engagement came as a bit of a shock, huh?"

"Basically." Annie didn't take her eyes from her father's vineyards.

"I remember what it was like to be eleven." Meredith's tone was soothing. "I had my first beau then. Before long, you'll understand what it's like to be in love."

"Me?" Annie was incredulous. "I don't even have twelve-year molars yet."

"Well, take it from someone who got molars very early in life," Meredith continued, "being in love is a fantastic mystery that takes a man and a woman—"

Annie cut her off. "I don't mean to be jerky when you're trying to be mushy, but I think I know what mystery my dad sees in you. You're young and sexy. And, hey, the guy's only human. But, if you ask me, marriage is supposed to be based on something more than sex. Right?"

Meredith's eyes went hard. "Boy, your father underestimates you."

"But you won't," Annie said. "Will you, Meredith?"

"This is the *real deal*, honey, and nothing you do is going to come between us." Meredith was getting angry. "I hate to break it to you, angel, but you're no longer the only girl in Nick Parker's life. Get over it."

Annie pretended to think aloud. "If this is the 'real deal,' then my dad's money has nothing to do with you wanting to marry him."

Meredith recoiled. It was a nice move, almost convincing. "I hope you're not suggesting I'm marrying your father for his money."

"I've seen *Cinderella* a few zillion times," Annie said. "I'd rather not end up scrubbing the floors while you're having breakfast in bed. If you catch my drift."

Meredith lost her remaining composure. "Okay, you listen and you listen good. I'm marrying your father in two weeks, whether you like it or not. I'd suggest you not tangle with me anymore. You're in way over your head. Is that clear?"

Annie leaned back, stared at Meredith and uttered one word. "Crystal."

Martin was puzzled by the incoming fax. It featured a roughly drawn picture of Sammy with a cartoon talk-bubble that said "911!" It wasn't really funny, though perhaps it was a joke. He took it with him into the dining room where he was serving wine.

Grandfather Charles checked the label. "Lovely wine, Martin."

"Thank you, sir." Martin filled Elizabeth's glass.

"May I have a sip?" It was Hallie.

Her mother warned her, "I don't think you're going to like it."

Expertly, Hallie swirled the wine, passed it under her nose, and finally took a sip. "If you ask me, the bouquet is a little robust for a Merlot," she pronounced. "But I'm partial to the softer California grape."

Everyone laughed. They thought she was kidding. As Martin refreshed Elizabeth's glass, Hallie saw the fax with the picture of Sammy. She had to bend so far to read it, she fell out of her chair. "Honey!" Elizabeth said. "Are you okay?"

"Had one sip too many," Hallie told her. "Just a touch woozy. I need a bit of air. Would it be okay if I stepped outside for a moment?"

Her mother excused her without thought, but her grandfather was more skeptical. "Woozy, huh?"

Once outside, Hallie hurried to a phone booth on the corner. Annie answered on the first ring. "Hal! I'm desperate! Dad's getting married!"

Hallie didn't believe her. "Waddya mean, getting married?"

Annie said, "I mean black tie, white gown, the whole enchilada."

"What?!?" Hallie cried.

"The wedding's in two weeks," Annie informed her, "so if there's any hope of getting Mom and Dad together, we've got to do it fast. I mean fast, *really* fast."

"Oh, this is awful." Hallie glanced around. A man was waiting to use the phone. He was half hidden behind a newspaper. "Mom and I are going to the theater tonight . . . I'll . . . I'll drop the bomb on her first thing in the morning."

"Good!" Annie was relieved. "Give Mom a kiss for me. Grandfather, too."

Hallie hung up and stepped from the booth. She bumped into the man who was waiting. "Oh, excuse me," she said. And then, "Uh-oh."

Grandfather Charles lowered the paper. "What do you say you and I take a little stroll in the park, young lady?"

From opposite sides of the earth that night, both girls wished upon a star. The next morning Hallie went to her mother's room. Elizabeth was wearing satin pajamas and speaking French on the phone while she sketched a wedding gown on a pad. When she was done, she called, "Come in."

Hallie crawled into bed and snuggled close. Elizabeth told her, "I have to finish this sketch and send it to Paris, then how about we have lunch and get lost at Harrods?"

Hallie was nervous. "I can't, Mom, sorry. I have to go out of town today."

Elizabeth thought Hallie was playing. "Where, may I ask, are you going?"

"I have to go see Annie." Hallie disappeared beneath the covers.

Her mother played along. "And where would Annie be?"

"In Napa, California, with her father, Nick Parker."

Chapter 15

"Annie and I met at camp and decided to switch places. I've dreamed of meeting you my whole life, and Annie felt the exact same way about Dad." The words tumbled out. "I hope you're not mad because I love you so much and I just hope one day you can love me as me and not as Annie."

"Oh, honey. I've loved you your whole life." Elizabeth pressed her cheek against that of her daughter. "Why didn't you tell me it was you all along?"

Hallie spoke through tears, "I was scared."

Martin was crying, too. He stood in the doorway with Grandfather Charles, sobbing his heart out. Gravely, Grandfather nodded his approval. He shut the door and Martin fell into his arms, heaving with emotion.

Inside the room, alone with her daughter, Elizabeth wiped away the tears. "I guess you'll have to switch us back now, huh?" Hallie asked her.

"Well, you do belong to your father and Annie belongs to me. . . ."

"His and Hers kids," Hallie said. "No offense, Mom, but this arrangement really sucks."

"I agree." Elizabeth shook her head. "It totally sucks."

Hallie had long been thinking, trying to decide what to

do. "I say we fly to Napa, see Annie and Dad, and work this thing out."

"I say you're right."

"Will you be nervous about seeing my dad again?" Hallie asked.

"I can handle seeing Nick Parker after all these years." Elizabeth's thoughts were far away. "People see their exes all the time, don't they? Not to worry, sweetheart. I'll take care of everything. Not to worry."

After the reality of the situation finally sank in, Elizabeth was singing a different tune. "I'm sorry. I can't handle this. I haven't heard from Nick Parker in over eleven years and suddenly I'm flying halfway across the world to see him. I'm not mature enough for this. If the man didn't make me so nuts, I'd still be married to him."

Martin simply inclined his head. With Elizabeth in such a mood, no one could get a word in edgewise. "We came up with this arrangement so we'd never see each other. Look at me. Have you ever seen me like this? Don't answer that."

Elizabeth was pacing, wearing sunglasses in the house and actually smoking, as she tried to figure out what to pack. "What if he doesn't recognize me? Be honest, Martin . . . how old do I look? Don't answer that. Hey, what am I worried about? He could be fat or bald. Or both."

Martin cleared his throat. "Actually, Hallie says her father is quite a hunk. And never remarried. Rather like yourself, madam."

Elizabeth rounded on him. "Martin! It just so happens

I'm not remarried by choice. I've had my opportunities. Not lately, of course. But I've had my share."

"Not lately," Martin declared.

"I just *said* that!" Elizabeth stopped short. "Hallie said he was a hunk, huh? He was rather dishy. The man had a smile that made me go weak in the knees. If you can imagine that."

When Hallie came in with an overnight bag, Elizabeth tried to pull herself together. "I'm all set, Mom," Hallie said.

"Me, too," Elizabeth claimed. "Almost. Not quite."

Hallie frowned. "Mom, your suitcase is totally empty."

"Oh. Right. Sorry." Elizabeth stubbed out the cigarette. "Did you speak with your father?"

"Uh, yeah." Hallie couldn't meet her eyes, or Martin's, but Elizabeth was too scattered to notice. "I just hung up, actually. He's really anxious to see you."

"Anxious-nervous, as if he's dreading it?" Elizabeth turned to face her. "Or anxious-excited, as if he's looking forward to it?"

"Anxious-excited," Hallie decided. "Definitely." Martin squinted at her in suspicion. "He'll meet us tomorrow at noon at the Stafford Hotel in San Francisco."

Her mother stared at her empty luggage. "Tomorrow? My, that's incredibly soon, isn't it? Well, honey, why don't you run downstairs and collect our tickets from your grandfather while I finish up here?"

The butler followed Hallie out. He whispered, "Liar, liar, pants on fire . . ." He couldn't add anything else, though, as Elizabeth was calling him back.

"Martin, I have a ridiculous, somewhat childish request." Elizabeth's tone was pleading. "Martin, you're more than a butler to me. You're like a lovable brother, who just happens to wait on us, and . . . anyway, I was wondering if . . . "

Martin finished for her. "If I'd accompany you to make the trip a bit easier?"

"Would you, Martin? I'd be incredibly grateful." Elizabeth relaxed. "And you don't even have to go as our butler. Just as a friend."

"Madame, I'd be honored," he said. "And, as a friend, may I say that if I were seeing my ex after eleven years, and if I had your legs—" Martin took a short black dress from the closet. "I'd wear this baby. You'll kill in it."

Now that she knew she *had* a grandfather, it was hard for Hallie to say good-bye. He hugged her and promised to come to Napa for Thanksgiving. She raised up on her tiptoes to kiss him. "Say hello to your father for me," he said.

"I will!" She got into the Bentley and waved and waved until she could no longer see him.

Chapter 16

It was noon by the clock at the Stafford Hotel, twelve o'clock in San Francisco. Meredith walked across the lobby with her parents. They were a smoothly polished couple. "He'll be here any minute," she said. "Be nice, Daddy. He's everything you ever wanted for me . . . and millions more."

Her father beamed his approval. "Then you know I'll be nice." The family had themselves a hearty laugh.

"There he is!" Meredith's face fell. "With the whole motley crew." Just behind Nick were Annie, Chessy, and to Meredith's amazement, Sammy. "Honey!" Meredith hissed. "A *dog* at the Stafford?"

Nick shrugged. "Hal begged me to bring him."

"You're such a . . . softy," Meredith managed, and Sammy snapped at her. "Good doggy," Chessy whispered. "Meredith? These are your folks?"

"Yes. Finally you all meet." Meredith linked her arm with Nick's. "Mom, Dad, this is my fiancé and the love of my life, Nicholas Parker."

"Hi, Nick." The mom's smile was huge. "I'm Vicki."

"And this is Nick's adorable daughter, Hallie," Meredith went on. "This entire prenuptial get together was her idea, I'll have you know." Meredith's mom smiled a little too broadly. "Hello, pet. You can call me Aunt Vicki."

Annie crossed her fingers behind her back, hoping she'd never have to.

Outside the Stafford a limousine pulled up, and Hallie and Martin emerged. Martin had to help the remaining passenger. Elizabeth was somehow a little tipsy. She took a miniature bottle of vodka from her purse and polished it off. "That was a great flight, wasn't it?" She tossed the bottle over her shoulder. "So quick."

Martin caught it before it hit the ground. "I've never seen you so *thirsty* before, ma'am."

"Would you believe, Marty, ol' mate, that I never tasted vodka before this trip?" Elizabeth hiccuped.

"Could have fooled me, ma'am."

Elizabeth peered at a young man in the entryway. "Hello, doorman. Oh, you scared me! I thought you were real for a minute."

Hallie was mumbling to herself. "I am in such major trouble here." She followed her mother to the reception desk and managed to keep her from ringing the bell over and over again. "Mom? Are you gonna be okay?"

"Absolutely. Never felt better in my life," Elizabeth assured her. "But, darling, I'm a bit confused. Have we landed yet?" Major trouble.

When Sammy caught a familiar scent, neither Annie nor Chessy could control him. Straining at his leash, the dog dragged them both away. Meredith was oblivious. She was saying, "Why don't we all go up to our rooms, freshen up, and then rendezvous for lunch?"

61

"Great," her father said. "We'll meet you at the bar in ten."

Meredith kissed his cheek, then turned to Nick. "Sweetheart, let's check out the Stafford honeymoon suite while we're here. I'll bet it's to die for."

On the other side of the hotel lobby, Hallie and Martin had gotten into an elevator. Elizabeth was lagging behind. "Oh, jeez," she said. "I forgot my purse."

Heading for the front desk, she bypassed an excited dog. Sammy was hot on the trail of his favorite girl. He jumped into the elevator and almost knocked Hallie down. As he licked her face, the doors slid shut. They were on their way.

Elizabeth snatched up her purse and returned to the bank of elevators just as Annie and Chessy arrived. Annie hadn't seen her mother since she'd left for camp. "Mom!" Annie hugged her tight.

Elizabeth didn't notice Chessy, and she thought Annie was Hallie. "You didn't have to wait for me." She was slurring. "I could've found the room by myself. Besides, I've got to make a pit stop. Go on, thweetie, I'll meet you upthstairs."

Annie watched her mother weave toward the restroom, and then she slapped her forehead. "She's drunk!" she told Chessy. "She never drinks more than one glass of wine, and she chooses today to be zonked!"

Chessy pressed the button for the elevator. "Let's just do what the woman says and meet her upthstairs."

After they had gone upstairs, Meredith and Nick came up to the same elevator bank. Meredith was nibbling on Nick's ear. When the doors opened and they walked in, she put her arms around him. "Alone at last."

Before the doors closed, Nick spotted Elizabeth. She was walking toward them. Nick's eyes went wide. Meredith was kissing him, kissing him thoroughly, so Nick couldn't say a word. Not knowing what else to do, Elizabeth waved.

Chapter 17

Furious, and suddenly much more focused, Elizabeth charged down the hallway. "Hallie Parker!" Two doors opened simultaneously. Annie stood in one doorway, Hallie in the other. "Stop that!" Elizabeth yelled. "I'm already seeing double!"

All at once, Elizabeth realized she was seeing the girls together for the first time. She immediately took both girls into her arms and held them tight. Then she looked from one to the other and then asked, "How could you do this to me?"

"May I suggest we take this little powwow inside?" Chessy interrupted. "Elizabeth, you probably don't remember me—"

Elizabeth remembered. "Chessy!"

Chessy smiled. "I knew I always liked you."

Once inside Elizabeth's suite, the girls sat side by side. Their mother glared at them both. "One of you, I don't know which one at the moment, but *one* of you told me that your father knew I was arriving here today."

Neither could meet her eyes. Elizabeth went on. "The man I just saw in the elevator had absolutely no idea he and I were on the same planet, let alone in the same hotel."

"You saw Dad already?" That was Annie.

"Yes, I did. The man went completely ashen. Like I was the bloody ghost of Christmas past." Elizabeth flopped down on the sofa. "Can one of you get something cold for my head?"

Elizabeth rubbed her temples. "Don't you think I've pondered what it was going to be like to see your father again? Me waving like an idiot while Nick Parker is wrapped in another woman's arms is not exactly the scenario I had in mind."

One of the twins handed her a wet washcloth, and Elizabeth put it to her forehead. "Furthermore, I've been lied to by my own children and I'd like to know why."

She closed her eyes and opened them to see Martin. The butler was wearing only a skimpy swimsuit. "Martin! What are you doing?"

"Going for a dip," he answered. "Do you mind?"

"No, no, that's perfectly perfect. "Elizabeth was being sarcastic. "Have fun, by all means, and at least put on a shirt."

Chessy stopped cold when she came into the room and saw Martin for the first time. "Oh," she said. "Hello. Hello."

"Hello, hello to you," he echoed and smiled. While they were introduced, he gallantly kissed Chessy's hand. *"Enchanté, mademoiselle."* Martin and Chessy stared into each others eyes for a long moment.

The twins giggled. They couldn't help it. This was way too good. "Girls!" Their mother called them to attention. "You were going to tell me why you lied and brought me here without telling your father."

"Were they?" Chessy quickly sidled toward the door.

"Why don't I just slip back into my room and check out the mini-bar situation?"

"Allow me to assist you?" Martin chimed in also trying to escape.

"Wait!" Elizabeth cried. "Does everyone know something I don't know?"

"Daddy's getting married," Annie blurted finally. "To . . . to Cruella De Vil." Elizabeth exhaled sharply. "Your father's a grown man," she said. "He's quite capable of deciding whom he wishes to marry."

"But she's awful. She's all wrong for him," Hallie insisted. "And the only way he won't marry her is—"

She broke off and Annie finished, "—is if he sees you again."

"Just a minute!" Their mother was putting it together. "You're not trying to fix me up with your father?"

"We are," Hallie said. "You're perfect for each other."

"A match made in heaven," Annie added.

"Hold it!" Elizabeth turned to Chessy and Martin. "You knew about this?" Their excuses were so silly that Elizabeth cut them short. "Let me say this loud and clear. Nick Parker and I have nothing in common anymore. Plus, in case you haven't noticed, he seems content with his leggy, tight-skirted, size-four fiancée."

She paused and stared hard at the twins. "I want you to explain to your father that I am here for one purpose, and one purpose only, and that is to switch you two back. Now, let's do what we have to do and be done with it. Understood?"

* * *

"No, I don't understand." In yet another room, Meredith was confronting Nick. He was acting strangely. It was as if he'd seen a ghost, and he wasn't making sense.

"I just need to go downstairs for a few minutes to clear my head." Nervously, he ran his fingers through his hair. "Then I'll meet you for lunch."

"Clear your head? Is something wrong?" Meredith was worried.

"I hope not. I mean, no, nothing," Nick said. "What could be wrong? We're getting married in ten days. Everything's perfect."

"We're still going ring shopping after lunch, right?"

"Ring shopping? Oh, for the funeral," he said. "I mean, for the wedding."

Meredith stamped her foot. "Funeral?"

"I'm kidding." Nick tried to laugh, but it was unconvincing. "Don't listen to me. I'll see you downstairs."

On his way down, Nick bumped into Annie and then into Hallie. But he was already too flummoxed to try to sort it out.

Chapter 18

Hallie had not yet met Meredith, so she had no way of recognizing the woman who stepped out of the elevator. Meredith snapped her compact shut and asked, "Have you seen your father?"

"You talkin' to me?"

"Who are you, De Niro?" Meredith was disgusted. "Yes, I'm talking to you."

Hallie realized then who she was. She sized Meredith up. "He went thataway, I think. You're really very pretty."

"Don't tell me you're going to break your rotten streak to be nice to me." Meredith zipped the compact into her purse. "If you see your father, tell him he's late and I'm waiting."

"Whatever you say," Hallie said. Under her breath she added, "Cruella."

Meredith went into the bar and sat on an empty stool. The bartender was preparing a thick red concoction. "This'll cure anything you've got," he was telling another customer. "Just don't ask what's in it."

Elizabeth regarded it doubtfully. "Okay. Here's to—" She glanced at the woman sitting nearby. "Here's to you. May your life be less complicated than mine."

Meredith tried to look gracious. "Thank you."

Elizabeth tossed down the red stuff, grimaced, and belched. "Excuse me. I apologize." She belched again. "I think I just drank tar."

Meredith snuck a peek when Elizabeth signed the bill. "You're Elizabeth James?" she inquired. "Elizabeth James the designer?"

"Guilty," Elizabeth admitted.

"I can't believe it! I just saw a wedding dress you designed and fell in love with it. I faxed your office, but they said you were out of town." She offered her hand. "I'm Meredith Blake. And this has got to be fate."

Nick squinted into the sun, searching the pool area for Elizabeth. "There you are!" Meredith's father hailed him. "We've been looking all over for you."

Meredith's mom was still smiling. "Nicholas, I think this hotel is perfect for the wedding. The more I see of it, the more I like it."

Nick wasn't listening. "Me, too. Absolutely." He scanned the crowd and finally saw his former wife.

"Tell me, dear," Meredith's mom rattled on, "how many guests will there be from your side of the family? Just a guesstimate."

"I'm not sure at the moment," Nick said. "I'll have to get back to you on that one." Like a man in a dream he started off toward Elizabeth. He sidestepped a few toddlers, nearly bumped into a waiter, then got tangled in Sammy's leash.

"Dad!" Annie yelled. "Watch out!"

Nick turned back, stumbled and splashed headfirst into

69

the pool. He was mad when he climbed out. He was not only embarrassed, he had scraped his cheek. But as he drew near to Elizabeth his anger faded. He smiled. "Hello, Liz."

Her knees went weak. She grabbed onto an umbrella for support. "Hello, Nick. Gosh. There you are. What do you know."

Nick pushed the wet hair from his eyes. "Is there something going on here I should know about? Obviously, I'm surprised to see you. I fell into the pool, but you don't seem all that stunned to see me."

"Let's not get too weird about this, okay?" she pleaded.

"It's a little late for that advice, as I stand here dripping wet. I don't see or hear from you in eleven years and suddenly you are here on the very day I—"

"Dad, I can explain why she's here." Annie had appeared at her mother's side.

Nick was surprised. "Hallie. You know who this is?"

"Actually, yes," Annie said in her own voice. "And actually, I'm not Hallie."

"Actually," Hallie broke in, "I am."

Nick stared at Annie, then Hallie, and Annie again. He swallowed with difficulty and turned to Elizabeth. "Both of them? Annie? Hallie?"

It was Annie who clued him in. "I guess you and Mom kind of think alike, because you both sent us to the same camp. We met there and the whole thing sort of just spilled out."

Elizabeth looked into his eyes. "They switched places on us, Nick."

"I wanted to know what you were like," Annie told him. "And Hallie wanted to know Mom. Are you angry?"

It was taking time to sink in. "Of course not." He hugged her hard. "I can't believe it's you. The last time I saw you, you had diaper rash. Look at you!"

"Quite grown-up and quite without a father," Annie said.

"And I'm headed into my crazy teenage years without a mother to fight with," Hallie added.

Nick was still piecing it together. "You mean, I've had Annie all this time. And Hallie . . . you've been in London. Come here, squirt." He embraced her as well.

"Mom's amazing, Dad," Hallie said. "I don't know how you ever let her go."

Elizabeth shushed her. She took a shaky breath. "Girls, why don't you let your father and me talk for a couple of minutes, okay?"

The girls both smiled as they turned to leave, "Sure. Take your time."

Chapter 19

"Ouch! I can't believe this . . . seeing them together . . . and seeing you. Ouch!" Elizabeth was tending to Nick's scraped cheek. "How are you, Lizzie? Or does everyone call you Elizabeth now?"

"Lizzie's fine," she said. "My dad still calls me Lizzie. I've been terrific."

He looked at her for a moment, then smiled. "You know, you haven't really changed at all."

"You thought I'd be fat and gray?"

"Well, maybe not gray," he teased. "Ouch!" Their eyes locked for a moment, when suddenly they heard: "There you are!" It was Meredith. Simultaneously, Nick and Elizabeth turned toward her. "Elizabeth designs wedding gowns," Meredith informed her bridegroom. "She's going to make my—"

Meredith broke off. The scene in front of her wasn't quite right. "How did you two meet? Nicky, why are you all wet?"

"I slipped," Nick replied. He turned to Elizabeth. "You're making my fiancée's wedding gown?"

Elizabeth shrugged. "I didn't know she was your fiancée."

Meredith looked from one to the other. "Am I missing something here?"

"Sweetheart?" Nick took her hand. "This is one small world."

Meredith's eyes narrowed. "How small?"

"Hey, Mer!" Meredith turned to see Hallie next to her. As if in stereo, another voice chimed in as well. "How ya doing?" Meredith turned the other way as Annie joined the group.

Meredith screamed twice at seeing double.

It took a while for Nick to explain it all—the former marriage, the twins, the meeting at the hotel. "The children arranged it?" Meredith had spoken through clenched teeth. "My, my, my. How sweet."

By late afternoon, she was still stewing. "I don't see why you have to have dinner with your ex-wife," she whined. "Why couldn't you just meet her in the lobby, discuss the custody, shake hands, and say good-bye? I'll tell you why. Because your daughters don't want me to marry you."

"That's not true." Nick leaned against the jewelry case.

"It's totally true. They see me as the evil stepmother." Meredith called to a saleswoman, "Can we have some help over here please? Can I try on the emerald cut? The big one? The bigger one? The biggest one?"

"Calm down," Nick told her. "The girls have never had a meal with both their parents in their entire lives. How could I say no?"

"Easily." She slipped the ring on her finger. "What do you think?"

Nick checked his watch. "I think I have to get dressed for dinner."

Meredith waved the ring beneath his nose. "Nicky?"

"If you love it," he said, "I love it."

Meredith threw her arms around him and said, "I love you." Behind his back, she admired the ring. And Nick, once again, glanced at his watch.

Dressed to the nines, Hallie and Nick emerged from the Stafford Hotel. "I've had enough surprises for one night," he was saying. "Just tell me where we're going."

"You're gonna love it, Dad," Hallie promised. "Trust me."

She hadn't told him anything. Nick was about to pursue it when he caught sight of Annie and his ex-wife. Elizabeth was wearing the black dress Martin had recommended. And it *was* killer. "Uh, hey!" Nick stammered. "Hi!"

"Hi," Elizabeth responded. "Do you have any idea where they're taking us?"

Nick looked at the girls, but they only smiled mysteriously. "Not a clue."

The taxi pulled up to a deserted pier. A lonely sound of a foghorn pierced the night. "This is where we're eating?" Nick raised his eyebrows.

Hallie pointed. "*That's* where we're eating."

A luxurious yacht was anchored a short distance away. It was strung with welcoming lights and bobbed gently in the bay. A skiff was waiting to take them aboard. Nick asked, "How exactly are we paying for this?"

"We pooled our allowances, Dad," Annie said. "Okay, Grandfather pitched in a bit." He gave her another look. "Okay, he pitched in a lot."

"C'mon!" When the skiff nudged up against the waiting boat, Hallie grabbed his hand. "You're gonna love it."

Near the rear of the yacht was a candlelit table. The San Francisco Bay Bridge formed a romantic backdrop. "The table's only set for two," Nick observed.

"That's the other part of the surprise," Annie said. "We're not joining you."

"But I am." Chessy's words emerged from the darkness. She stepped forward, wearing tropical white. "I'll be your server tonight. No wisecracks, please."

Martin appeared behind her. He held a bottle of champagne. "May I offer a taste of bubbly in hopes that you'll get a bit snickered and won't can this lovely lady and myself for following the orders of two audacious eleven-year-olds?"

"Mood music," Chessy ordered. "If you please."

The girls fiddled with buttons, dimmed the lights, and filled the night with music. "Just relax," Annie said. "Sail through time . . . "

Hallie crossed her fingers for luck. " . . . back to yester-year."

Chapter 20

It was a night of drifting clouds and twinkling city lights. "They're recreating the night we met," Nick said. "The boat . . . the music . . . "

"The help." Chessy pointed to herself.

"It's incredibly sweet." Elizabeth indicated the life preserver hanging on the wall. It had a homemade sign that read: QE2.

Nick stared at it. "Martin? I think I'll have that drink."

Martin poured and motioned to Chessy and they both disappeared. Nick raised his glass to Elizabeth. "To tell you the truth, I haven't been on a boat since the *QE2*."

"Neither have I." A breeze drifted against her cheek, lifted a lock of her hair.

Nick was having some trouble with breathing. "Well, then, here's to—"

"—our daughters," Elizabeth finished for him.

That wasn't exactly what he'd been thinking, but it was good enough. "Our daughters," he conceded. "I always see you in Hallie. Something about her eyes . . . "

"I always see you in Annie," she said. "Something about her smile . . . "

An awkward moment came on then. Nick caught a glimpse of the girls spying on them through matching portholes. "Now I know how a gold fish feels."

He lowered his voice. "Sometime, if we're ever together alone, maybe we could talk about what happened between us. It all feels a bit hazy to me now. It ended so fast."

"It started so fast," Elizabeth said.

He grinned at her. "Now *that* part I remember perfectly."

Through another porthole, Martin and Chessy were checking in on them periodically. "Looks like things are heating up nicely." Martin rubbed his palms together. "I'd say it's safe to serve the vichyssoise."

"You ladle," Chessy told him. "I'll serve. Or I'll ladle, and you can serve, or you can—" The butler was standing very near her, looking into her eyes. They stood there, neither wanting to move.

Outside, Elizabeth and Nick were catching up. "You've done so well," she was saying. "Your dream of owning your own vineyard actually came true."

"And, hey, how about you?" he interrupted. "Always drawing on napkins and newspapers? Now you're a major designer . . . pretty impressive."

"Yeah, it's amazing." Elizabeth sipped her champagne. "We both got where we wanted to go." Nick considered that. Did they?

When Chessy finally arrived with the vichyssoise, they were discussing the girls. "Now that they've met," Nick was saying, "we can't keep them apart."

"I guess I could keep them half the year," Elizabeth said. "And you could—"

"Guys!" Chessy protested. "They can't go to two schools a year. That's nuts."

77

Nick gave Chessy a look and she quickly made an exit.

Elizabeth reconsidered. "Okay. I keep them both for a year, and you could—"

"Liz, that's why we came up with the solution we have."

"*That's* why?" She was surprised. "Really? I thought it was because we decided never to see each other again."

He shook his head. "Not *we*, Liz."

She looked down. "That part's become hazy for me, too, over the years."

"You don't remember the day you packed?" His eyes were very bright.

"No, that day I remember perfectly." She thought about it and asked, "Did I hurt you when I threw that . . . what was it . . . ?"

"It was a hair dryer."

"Oh, right," she said. "Were you hurt? I've often wondered."

Nick rubbed his shoulder. "Let's put it this way," he joked. "I'll never pitch for the Yankees." He picked up his spoon then put it down. "So how come you never got remarried? I always figured you'd be married with a new family, and . . . "

"No," she said. "No, no, no, no. I guess I realized a long time ago that marriage just wasn't for me."

"That's a lot of no's." Nick suddenly felt very sad. "You know, I may never be alone with you again . . . so . . . about the day you packed. Why'd you do it?"

"We were so young, we each had tempers, we said

foolish things." Elizabeth sighed. "So I packed. I got on my first 747. And you didn't come after me."

He looked at her—realizing something for the first time. "I didn't know you wanted me to."

For lack of something better to do, she picked up her own spoon and pretended to taste the soup. "It really doesn't matter anymore. Look, let's put a good face on for the girls and get this show on the road." She avoided his eyes.

Nick opened his mouth, then hesitated. "Okay," he said. "Sure. Let's get this show on the road."

The next morning, Martin dealt with the luggage while Elizabeth signed the bill at the Stafford. "All set then," she announced. "Now, where's Annie?"

"I just called," Martin said. "She's on her way down."

Nick, too, was checking out. Together, he and Elizabeth went over the plans they'd made. Hallie would go to London for Christmas. Annie would fly to the ranch for Easter. It was all very fair and no one was happy, least of all the girls.

When the twins entered the lobby, they were dressed identically. No one could possibly tell them apart.

Chapter 21

Elizabeth stared from one to the other and back again. "Annie? What are you doing in those clothes? Honey, we've got a plane to catch."

Hallie smirked. "Are you sure I'm Annie?"

"Of course I'm sure," Elizabeth claimed. Though she really wasn't.

"Girls, this is completely unfunny," Nick said. "You're gonna make your mother miss her plane."

Both smiled, exactly alike. Both turned in unison when Elizabeth called their names. Nick examined them together and said, "This one's Hallie, I'm positive."

He had chosen Annie. The real Hallie teased him— speaking with a proper British accent, "I hope you're right, Dad. You wouldn't want to send the wrong kid all the way back to London."

"Here's our proposition," Annie began. "We go back to Dad's house, pack our stuff, and the four of us leave on the camping trip."

"The *four* of us?" Elizabeth couldn't believe her ears.

"And when you bring us back," Hallie continued, "we'll tell you who's who."

Elizabeth tried to take control of the situation. "Or you do as we say and I take one of you back with me to London," she threatened, "whether you like it or not . . . "

The plane to London lifted into the sky, empty of either twin. Meanwhile, back at the ranch, four sleeping bags were tossed into the back of Nick's sport utility. Meredith watched unhappily. "And what am I supposed to do for three days? Sit home and knit?"

When Elizabeth emerged from the house with a backpack, Meredith's mood got ugly. "Nicky? What's *she* doing here?"

"That was the deal," he told his fiancée. "The four of us together—"

"What are you?" Meredith shrieked. "The Brady Bunch? This is ridiculous!"

"Hi, Meredith." Elizabeth's greeting was cautious. "Everything okay?"

"No! As a matter of fact, it isn't!" Meredith's voice rose. "It is not okay!"

"I agree. The ex-wife in the next sleeping bag is a bit odd." Elizabeth seemed sympathetic. "I must insist you come with us. Really."

Nick started to protest and Elizabeth wouldn't hear it. "Nick, I messed up your entire weekend. It's the least I can do."

Meredith was wearing skintight and skimpy black workout gear when she got into the front passenger side of the truck. "Dad?" Hallie asked. "What's Meredith doing here?"

He slid behind the driver's wheel. "Your mother invited her. Be nice."

81

But instead of getting in back with the twins, Elizabeth closed the door. "Okay! Have fun everybody!"

Nick lowered his sunglasses. "Liz? What are you doing?"

Her reply was purposely innocent. "I really think you and Meredith need some time alone before the big day. And it will be her chance to get to know the girls. After all, starting next week, they'll be half hers."

Elizabeth blew kisses all around. "Have fun, you all!"

Chessy joined Elizabeth to watch the car pull away. Chessy was shaking her head. "I would pay good money to see that woman climb a mountain."

The mountains were rugged and beautiful, the trail was steep, and Meredith was having problems. She was huffing and puffing, her nose was sunburned, and she kept falling behind. "I'm going to kill my trainer. He says I'm in such good shape. I can't believe people actually do this for fun."

Meredith plopped down on a rock and Nick came up beside her. "Hold on, girls!" he called. "We're stopping."

Hallie trotted back down the path. "Again? At this rate—"

"Meredith isn't used to the altitude," her father said. "Just chill, okay?"

While Nick was talking to Hallie, Annie slipped several large rocks into Meredith's backpack. Meredith didn't notice. "Hand me my Evian . . . I can't move."

A small lizard was sunning nearby. Annie picked it up and let it cling to Meredith's water bottle. "Here you go, Mer."

Meredith lifted the bottle to her lips and found herself

eye-to-eye with the lizard. She screamed and threw it away, falling off the rock as she did.

"Honey!" Nick asked, "Are you okay?"

Annie collected the bottle and the little lizard. "He won't hurt you, Mer." She held the lizard up to Meredith's face.

"Get it away from me!" she yelled. "It's a lizard. Ugh! How can you touch it? Put it down!" Without either adult seeing her, Annie complied by putting the lizard down on top of Meredith's head.

"Why don't I take the lead?" Nick suggested. "You two help Meredith."

He left Meredith muttering, "Sure you're going to help me . . . right over a cliff."

"Good idea," Hallie said to Annie. "See any cliffs?"

Meredith groaned as she raised the rock-filled backpack, but refused their assistance. "One more trick and I promise to make your lives miserable from the day I say 'I do.'"

"Whatever you say, Cruella," Hallie said. Along with Annie, she hurried to catch up with her father.

Meredith whipped around to face the girls. "What did you call me?"

"Nothing," Hallie called back over her shoulder, "not a thing, Cruella." Her face took on a gleam of mischief. "Oh, by the way, Mer? I think there's something on your head."

Meredith reached up and discovered the lizard. She screamed a bloodcurdling scream and the frightened lizard ran down the side of her face right into her mouth. It's little body wiggled and squirmed and Meredith realized what was happening. Gagging, coughing, eyes bulging, Meredith finally spit it out.

When Nick questioned the girls, they were sweetly angelic, totally blameless. "What did we do, Dad? We were with you."

It was as if they had halos over their heads.

Chapter 22

"Please work. Please. Please work." But no matter what buttons Meredith pushed, her trusty cellular phone was out of its range. Just ahead, she could see Annie and Hallie. They were crouched over, examining something on the ground.

Annie pretended not to hear Meredith's approach. "I didn't know they had mountain lions up here!" she exclaimed.

"Yeah, the place is crawling with them." Hallie winked at Annie. "An old mountain guide once showed me how to keep them away." She took up two sticks and clacked them together. "Do this, and they'll never come near you."

As the girls disappeared down the path, Meredith stooped to pick up two sticks. Clacking one stick against the other, she followed. She was so nervous about the mountain lions that she didn't see the gopher hole in front of her. She clacked the sticks twice, stepped into the hole and tumbled halfway down the mountain.

The night held clear stars and a campfire. Meredith had refused to eat dinner. She sulked by the fireside, swatting at mosquitoes and rubbing lotion on her arms. "You sure you don't want some trout, Mom?" Annie asked her. "Is that okay, by the way? If we start calling you Mom?"

"I think I would prefer it if you called me Meredith. And, no, thank you, for the thousandth time, I do not eat trout. What are we having for breakfast?"

"Trout." The threesome chimed in. Nick was apologetic. "C'mon, it's part of the experience."

"What's the other part? Being eaten to death by mosquitoes?" Meredith swatted another. "You'd think they actually liked this stuff."

Nick took the lotion, smelled it, tipped some out on the palm of his hand. "You're going to attract every mosquito in the state with this. It's sugar and water. Where did you get it?"

Meredith glared at the twins. "That's it! I'm taking one large sleeping pill and going to bed." On her way to the tent, she picked up a pair of sticks and clacked them together.

"Meredith? What are you doing?" Nick was puzzled.

"I don't want the mountain lions—" Meredith broke off. She realized she'd been had. "There are no mountain lions up here, are there?"

"No." Nick shook his head. Deliberately, Meredith waltzed over, tossed the sticks in the fire and gave Nick a very long, luscious kiss. Both girls looked away.

After she had zipped herself into her tent, Nick rounded on his daughters. "I'm telling you guys, lay off. This isn't her thing, okay? Just cool it."

The sleeping pill was working. Meredith barely moved when the girls dragged her air mattress down to the lake.

86

With Meredith aboard, it was heavy, but they managed to launch it and watch it float away. Hallie bade her good night, "Sweet dreams . . . Mommie Dearest."

Drifting peacefully, Meredith slept soundly until dawn the next morning. She flopped one arm into the water and woke up. There was a bird perched on her nose. She screamed and screamed again. "Niiiiiiiiiiiiickyyyyyy!"

The sound resounded off the mountain peaks. Still mostly asleep, Nick peered out the door of his tent. He saw his fiancée thrashing around on the air mattress in the middle of the lake. He rubbed his eyes. "Oh, man . . . "

Meredith tried to stand but immediately fell backward into the water. She splashed to shore, sloshed up the bank, and stormed over to Nick. "What's going on?" Nick asked, trying to keep his tone neutral.

"Here's what's going on! The day we get married is the day I ship those brats off to Switzerland. Get the picture? It's me or them. Take your pick."

Nick's response was one syllable. "Them."

She stared at him in bewilderment. "Excuse me?"

He spelled it out. "T-H-E-M. Them. Get the picture?"

When the campers pulled up in front of the ranch house, Elizabeth rushed out to greet them. "Back so soon? Did you have fun?"

Hallie's smile was wan. "I wouldn't go right to 'fun.'"

"We've been punished through the end of the century," Annie said.

"Starting right now!" Nick's face was mock stern.

Someone was missing. "Where's Meredith?" Elizabeth asked.

87

"We played a couple of harmless tricks on her," Hallie told her mother. "And she kind of freaked out a little."

"A little? A little!" Nick showed Elizabeth the engagement ring. "She threw this at my head! At least it's smaller than a hair dryer."

"Oh, jeez, this is all my fault." Elizabeth pretended remorse. "If I hadn't suggested she go along—"

"Suggested? Tricked her would be more like it," Nick corrected her. "Like mother . . . like daughters."

"I'm really sorry," Elizabeth said.

"We are too, Dad." That was Annie.

He gestured toward the stairs. "Up to your room!" he commanded. "Go!"

When they were gone, he grinned at Elizabeth. "I gotta remember to thank them someday."

Slowly, softly, she smiled back.

Chapter 23

"Where is Chessy? I'm starving!"

"She and Martin went off on a picnic around noon," Elizabeth told him, and then she added with a small smile, "Noon—yesterday."

Nick glanced up with amusement and answered her with his best Cary Grant imitation, "Who would have thought . . . my nanny and your butler? So, anyway, how about I whip us up something to eat?"

Elizabeth was surprised. "You know how to cook now?"

He shrugged. "I can make pasta, and pasta, and—"

"Pasta sounds good," she said.

Nick went upstairs to shower, shave, and change clothes. When he passed by the girls' room, Hallie exclaimed, "Wow! You look nice. Where are you going?"

Firmly, Nick shut their door. "Good night, ladies!"

The kitchen smelled of nice things. Nick took an appreciative sniff. "Smells good in here," he announced.

Elizabeth turned to smile at him. "Really? I'm just boiling water."

"Then it must be you." He lined up several wine glasses on the counter. "What are you in the mood for—white or red?"

"I think . . . red."

"Follow me," Nick told her. He led her down into his private cellar. The space was illuminated by lanterns and the walls were lined with bottles of wine. "Did you know I also collect wine? I'm a man of limited interests."

Elizabeth laughed. Nick took a bottle from the rack and held it out to her. "Here's a 1921 Burgundy, maybe the best Burgundy ever." He dusted off another very old bottle. "You'll appreciate this one."

She peered at the label. "*VJ Day . . . 1945*. Incredible."

Nick pointed out some other bottles. "This is the same wine my parents served at their wedding, a 1952 Bordeaux. And here's one that took me years to track down."

Elizabeth read out loud, "*Where Dreams Have No End . . . 1983*."

"It's the wine we drank at our wedding." He observed her closely. "I now have every bottle in existence."

"You do?" Elizabeth had a lump in her throat.

"I do," he said quietly.

"Can we open one?"

"You're the only one I'd drink it with."

Elizabeth's eyes filled with tears. "You okay?" he asked her.

"Just got a little dust in my eye," she lied.

He held out his arms. "I can offer you a clean sleeve."

Elizabeth shook her head. "No, no, I'm fine. Really. All better."

Very gently, he said, "You don't always have to be so brave, you know."

"Oh, but I do, actually . . . " Her voice trailed off and she closed her eyes. Nick was about to kiss her. But the sound of a car on the gravel drive split the two apart. Elizabeth pulled herself together. "That will be Chessy."

"She has a key," Nick said. He tried to hold on to the moment, but when Chessy started calling to them, Elizabeth hesitated but then answered, "We'll be right up!"

She climbed the steps from the wine cellar into the kitchen. "Welcome back!" Elizabeth called. Nick looked at the bottle of wine in his hand. It was the special one, Elizabeth's wine. He put the bottle into a cabinet and sadly closed the door.

A steady rain fell the next morning. "Okay, then, I guess that's that. We're really off this time!" Elizabeth was attempting to be cheerful as the last suitcase was loaded into the waiting taxi.

No one backed her up. Martin and Chessy hugged under an umbrella and vowed to see each other for Christmas. The girls clung together. Nick just stood there with his hands in his pockets.

The rain came down harder. The perfect weather for an unhappy departure. The cab driver slammed the trunk. Nick kissed Elizabeth on the cheek. "Take care of yourself."

"I will," she promised. "You, too."

Chapter 24

It was raining in London, too. The Bentley passed down streets that were gray and wet. The dull mood matched Annie's and Elizabeth's emotions exactly. They each looked out the windows of the car and didn't speak.

In front of the town home, Martin helped them with their luggage. He held an umbrella over their heads and opened the front door.

Elizabeth dropped the bag she was carrying into the empty foyer. "Hello!" she called. "Anyone home?"

Into the answering silence, Annie shouted, "Grandfather?"

"I'll check the study," her mother said.

There was someone sitting at the desk, hidden behind a copy of the *Financial Times*. Elizabeth said, "Hey, stranger . . . "

The newspaper was lowered and Elizabeth was shocked to see Hallie. "Did you know the Concord gets you here in half the time?"

Annie was stunned to see her twin. "What are you doing here?"

Hallie was enjoying herself. "It took us around thirty seconds after you left to realize we didn't want to lose you two again."

"We?" That was Elizabeth.

"We." The answer was deep and heartfelt. Elizabeth whirled to see Nick. "I made the mistake of not coming after you once, Lizzie," he said. "And I wasn't going to do it again. No matter *how* brave you are."

He smiled at her and her knees went weak. As he moved toward her she started talking faster and faster. "I suppose you expect me to cry hysterically and fall into your arms and say we'll figure this whole thing out—this bicontinental relationship with daughters being raised here and there and you and I picking up where we left off and growing old and living happily ever after?"

He nodded. "Yes, to all of the above. Except you don't have to cry hysterically."

Her tears spilled down. "Oh, yes . . . I do!"

Nick took her face in his hands and they kissed a kiss worth waiting for.

Annie fell back into a chair, thrilled beyond belief. Hallie slid down the wall that was holding her up. She was totally amazed. "We did it. We actually did it!"

Happily Ever After . . .

Rose petals drifted and tossed in the white wake of a luxury liner, the Queen Elizabeth 2. Annie and Hallie, dressed as flower girls, scattered more petals overboard and watched happily as they floated through the air. Somewhere aboard the ship a wedding reception was in full swing. Martin had surprised everyone by kneeling before Chessy and presenting her with a diamond engagement ring. Meanwhile, on the dance floor, Nick and Elizabeth, husband and wife, once again, were locked together, dancing, gazing into each other's eyes. Although Hallie and Annie had never known it, this was the night they had been waiting for their entire lives.